Little Wolf, Forest Detective

First American edition published in 2001
by Carolrhoda Books, Inc.
published by arrangement with
HarperCollinsPublishers Ltd, London, England

Carolrhoda Books, Inc.
A division of Lerner Publishing Group
241 First Avenue North
Minneapolis, MN 55401 U.S.A.

Website address: www.lernerbooks.com

Library of Congress Cataloging-in-Publication Data

Whybrow, Ian.
Little Wolf : forest detective / by Ian Whybrow; illustrated by Tony Ross.
p.   cm.
Summary: Through a series of letters to his parents, Little Wolf relates his adventures as a
member of Yelloweyes Forest Detective Agency, crime solvers of the Frettnin Forest, as they
investigate a series of mysterious disappearances.
ISBN: 1–57505–413–2 (lib. bdg. : alk. paper)
[1. Detectives—Fiction. 2. Wolves—Fiction. 3. Mystery and detective stories.]
I. Ross, Tony, ill. II. Title.
PZ7.W6225 Lg 2001
[Fic]—dc21
00–012676

Manufactured in the United States of America
1 2 3 4 5 6 – SB – 06 05 04 03 02 01

Little Wolf,
Forest Detective

Ian Whybrow
Illustrated by Tony Ross

 Carolrhoda Books, Inc., Minneapolis

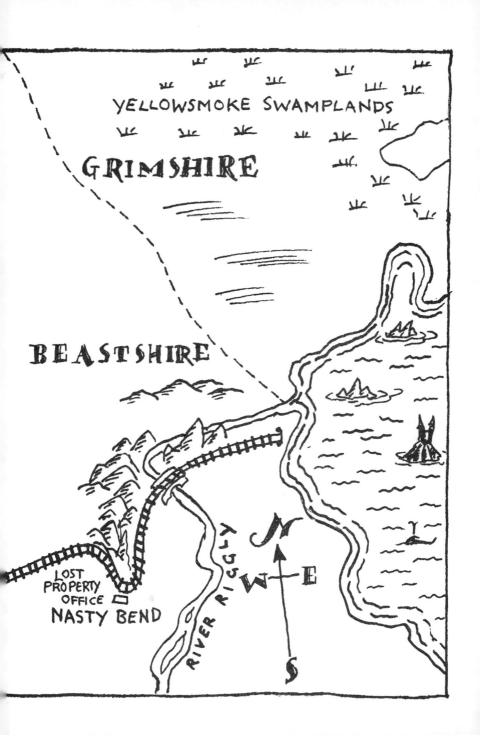

YELLOWEYES FOREST DETECTIVE AGENCY

FRETTNIN FOREST, BEASTSHIRE

(Not Haunted Hall School any more, hem hem Mister Mailman)

The office with the big desk in it

Dear Mom and Dad,

Please please please PLEEEZ don't make me come home to Murkshire to live in the lair with you and Smells. Whyo Y can't I stay here in Frettnin Forest with Yeller, Stubbs, and Normus? Because we like being detectives. It is good. Stubbs has made us nifty badges with his clever beak, saying YFDA (for Yelloweyes Forest Detective Agency, did you know that?):

7

Also, for our door he has done a nice new ~~sing sine~~ notice, saying:

We are good solvers, xcept for Smells. His brane is 2 small, plus he did not want to be in the YFDA. He got all feddup and lairsick, remember? That is Y he went back to Murkshire to live in the lair with you and to be your darling baby pet, yes? So, not my fault.

PLEEEZ, make him stay there. We do not want him back messing up our detective stuff. Like sitting on the fingerprint pad and doing bottomprints on my notebook. Also, he is selfish, saying nobody else can be the handcuffer, only him.

PLEEEZ.

Yours hopingly,

Little Wolf

My room

Dear Mom and Dad,

You did not say much to my last letter, only *hmmph* and *grrrr,* and *where is Uncle Bigbad's ghost? Find him quick, or else!!!*

We have been looking and looking, but no luck yet. Still, I have made you nice pics of what's in our detective kit so you will be more cheery. Yeller sent for it from *Wolf Weekly* (cheap). It is like this:

DETECTIVE KIT

Magnifying glass

Pawprint set

Handcuffs

Detective notebook with stickers like
INTERVIEW NOTES and CLUE
NOTES and EVIDENCE and
THINKY-OUT PAGE

Sharp pencil with earclip

Flashlight, to help
yellow eyes see in the dark

Penknife for sharp work

By the way, you ask what new cases we
have to solve? Answer: allsorts, but they are
confidenshul, private, can't say anything,
hem, hem.

Yours acely,

L.B. Wolf
Co-Cheef detective, YFDA

Dear Mamong et Parp-parp (french),

No, we have not found Mister Twister yet. Yes, I remember he has shamed the name of Wolf by being a kidnapper and ghostnapping Uncle Bigbad inside his bottle. But do not fret and frown, we will solve this case soonly, easy cheesy. (Probly.) But now we are a little busy doing Tips for Tecs to help us. Do you like them?

TIPS FOR FOREST TECS

🐾 *Practiss magnifying, pawprinting, handcuffing, sharpening (pencils), and shortpaw writing*

🐾 *Use your brute instinct*

🐾 *Use your keen beastly senses, such as eyes, ears, nose, and taking a good lick*

Find clues

Write about them in your notebook — quick, but no smudjis

Have a good think

Do plans for fast getaways

Then you will be an ACE Forest Detective and case solver, arrroooo!

Good, huh?

Yours cheefly,
   L. Wolf (son)

Shadow of my best tree

Dear Mom and Dad,

You keep asking what is the point of being your son if I do not blab my secret cases to my mom and dad? Oh, OK then. I will tell about just 1, but keep it in the lair. It is called "The Case of the Ants' Lost Soccer Shoes." Now I will tell you about the solving part.

The captain of Ants United came under our office door wearing his captain's shorts with his number on them (Number 9999999). He said antly, "Hello. Somebody has pinched all my team's soccer shoes. Can you detect who dunnit?" Normus said, "Yes, and I will bash them up for you." But Yeller and Stubbs and me said, "No need for bashing, Normus. Just for adding up, plus using your keen beastly senses."

So Normus said, "Okay then. How many shoes got pinched?" And the captain said, "All of them." That was a hard sum to figure, because of having to times all the ants by an ant's number of feet. But Yeller got the answer: 11 x 6 = 66. Then Normus said to the ant, "Wait, do you have any reserves?"

Good thing he said that, because the answer was yes, 1. That made 72 shoes pinched. And guess what? We solved who the stealer was! Arrroooo for the YFDA!

And now:

NEW MYSTERY CRIMES OF FRETTNIN FOREST

1) 13 pups, chicks, cubs, fledgies, etc. have gone missing from Frettnin Forest in 2 days.

2) Plus much treasure keeps getting robbed.

3) And reports are in of strange, spookly small things seen in the night.

It's all good, because it means lots more detecting for us. So watch out, all you kidnappers, robbers, and small spookles, because we have a detective kit and we can find out WHODUNNIT!

Yours trackingly,

L.B. Wolf

Co-cheef Detective, YFDA

Under dinner table (for cozyness, hmmm)

Dear Mom and Dad,

About "The Case of the Ants' Lost Soccer Shoes," I forgot to finish, sorry. The solving part was, we got out our magnifying glasses and had a good look around the hill where the ants live, going *stare, stare.*

Anycase, quite soonly we spotted many small tracks. We followed these, crawlingly, to a rotted log. And guess what we found hiding under the bark? A centipede wearing 72 soccer shoes! Stubbs can speak Insect, so he said, "Ark Squark Crark?" etc. meaning arkscuse me, small crook, are you warking for Mister Twister the Farks? Or are you warking alone as a stealer? Also, have you seen the ghost of Bigbad Wolf inside a bottle by any small chance?

The centipede said (insect voice), "You caught me, fellas. But I have not seen a big bad ghost, and no, I do not work for Mister Twister. Also, I am not a crook, really. I just wanted to do loud riverdancing and get faymuss. By the way, I taste horrible. Hint, hint."

Then he tried to do a fast getaway, but he tripped over his shoelaces and got captured, har, har. So, well done, us.

Yours Xplainingly,

Littly

P.S. He Xcaped soonly, boo, shame. Must get smaller handcuffs.

Up the troutpool, the chilly part

Dear Mom and Dad,

We had a good wet hunt for Mister Twister and Uncle Bigbad's ghost today, so I bet you are going, "Pat pat, well done, our cub." Yeller's Big Ideer was to swim down and look at Lake Lemming's bottom. Because you never know, Mister Twister is crafty enuff to hide down there. We saw some nice bubbles, and Normus caught a nice fishy lunch (yum, yum, tasty). But no crooks or ghosts inside bottles, boo, shame.

19

The ants' soccer team came over today saying we can be best friends and they will give us a kick around any time. Good, huh? Also, today we got a hansum reward because we found a lost froghopper in the long grass and took him back to his mom. She was so happy that she gave us some cuckoo spit. So now we have some nice foam to go on cups of hot chocklit. Yum, yum, tasty!

Yours yawnly,

Laaah Waaaah Zzzzzz

Dear Mom and Dad,

It is not my fault that Smells is jealous of my adventures. He always gets jealous. So go on, make him stay with you, hmmm? Stroke, stroke. Also, you are not being fair, saying *grrrrr*, you bet we do not earn much money being detectives because we cannot find my own dead uncle, even. It's true we are not rich yet, BUT (big but) what about all that gold I had in my safe till Smellybreff got some gunpowder and blew it to small smithers? That made my gold go scattering all over Frettnin Forest.

Never mind. Guess what? Stubbs found 3 gold coins high up in some nests yesterday! Arrroooo! So, well done, our Flying Squad. Good searching.

Now I will tell you more about what needs solving.

KIDNAPS

The Case of the Small Missing Moose
The Case of the 3 Bunnies that Hopped It
The Case of the 4 Pinched Hedgepiglets
The Case of the Lost Lion Cub
The Case of the 4 Disappeared Ducklings

Also

ROBBINGS

The Case of the Jackdaw's Jewels
The Case of the Weasel's
Gold Watch

SPOOKLY HAUNTINGS

The Case of the
Green Bubble that
Floats in the Nighttime

Ooo-er! What is happening? Where have all the small brute beasts gone? Who pinched the jewels and the watch? What comes floating in the night like a green bubble? Do not fear and fret, do not get wurrid, the YFDA will find out soon. Arrroooo!

Yours yellow-eyedly,

P.S. Mom always says yellow eyes are friends with the dark, right? So look out clues, we are after you, even with all the lights out!

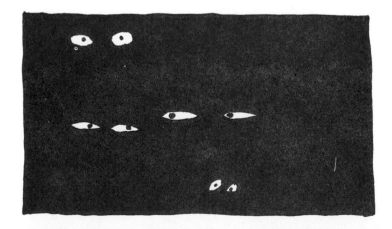

Sulking corner

Dear Mom and Dad,

Thank you for your harsh letter saying we are not truly detectives but you know somebody who is.

You say this somebody is not called a detective, but a Private Investigator which is a lot more cheefly. And he told you magnifying glasses are silly. He has all hi-tech tools for detecting, and he is called Furlock Holmes-Wolf. And he is faymuss because he solved "The Hard Case of the Slippery Chicks."

Now I feel all jealous.

Yours unpraisedly,

L. Wolf

*My desk (tidy, with all pencils sharp and
pointing same way)*

Dear Mom and Dad,

Very busy work today using brute instinct
and beastly senses. I will copy some pages
from our notebooks so you can say, hmm,
nice detecting you cubs.

YFDA INTERVIEW NOTES
(Private: keep out, smells, or else)

TIME   Case 1

early

DETECTIVE ON CASE

N. Bear

TIME OF INTERVIEW

Just after the sun jumped up.

WITNESS STATEMENT OF

Mrs. Duck, Tidynest, The Reeds, Lake
Lemming (the deep end).

"I was bobbing up and down counting my babies like you do. I never seen feather nor beak of nobody, only that nice gingery man with a mask on his face and a sort of fur badge on his front. He was holding a bag of crumbs. Then I noticed all my fluffies was gorn. Gorn! Oh woe is me, etc."

PLAN

Normus will go hunting in Lake Lemming area for gingery man with mask (a bit suspish) and furry badge. Plus 4 small ducks with fluff on them.

Case 2

DETECTIVE ON CASE

Yeller Wolf

TIME OF INTERVIEW

Just after snacktime

WITNESS STATEMENT OF

Mr. and Mrs. Lion,
Anywhere we feel like, Parching Plain.
"A traveling knifegrrrinder with squinty eyes came pushing his grrrrinder

over our hunting grrround. We noticed he was wearing a fur brrrrooch and he smelled minty. He said he had a special offer on claw sharrrpening, so we thought, why not? It was just after he went that we noticed our small cub was not asleep in his patch of long grrrrass. We rrreckon he was cubnapped."

PLAN

Yeller to Parching Plain to track minty suspect with fur brooch, pushing knifegrinder. Also looking for kidnapped cub called Pounce (left ear chewed).

Case 3

DETECTIVE ON CASE
S. Crow

TIME OF INTERVIEW
Ark past 2

WITNESS STATEMENT OF
Mrs. Hedgehog, Heapoleaves, Beech Grove, Frettnin Forest.
"A gingery gypsy it was, selling clothespins. With big spots. On her hanky.

She had a spotty hanky, you understand.
Her clothespins were not spotty. I
noticed she smelled minty and she had
a fur thingy pinned to her blouse. Is
that a help?

Snuffle, snuffle. Excuse me. I am upset.
I am always telling my hogglets never
to take slugs from a stranger! But it
was just too tempting for my little
cheeky chestnuts. Now they have been torn
from me. You must find them for me,
Mister Defective. I will pay anything.
Slugs, snails, worms, you name it."

PLAN

Flying Squad (Stubbs) to do Air search
for suspect with special GO CROW!
message on flying helmet.

GO CROW

Case 4

Co-Cheef Tec's Case (V. hard. Needs xtra keen beastly powers by me, hem, hem)

PLAN

To detect who robbed the jewels plus the gold watch from the jackdaw and weasel. My keen beastly ears, eyes, nose, etc. tell me that jackdaw and weasel are making up fibs, just so I will find rich things for them. They hope I will say, "Da-daaah! Look at this shiny stuff I have found. Are they yours by any chance, hem, hem?" So then they can pretend, saying, "Oh defnly, lovely, yes those are my treasures."

Yours R U kiddingly,

Your Little
Tracker

29

Dear Mom and Dad,

I know you like a good fib, so look at these whoppers I wrote down in my notebook by shortpaw (quck wrtin):

Me (detectively): Tll me Mistr Jckdaw, whr did you hde yr jewels? Ws it in a gd hidy-hole?

Jackdaw (harshly): I tuckd ma sprkly jools nder a lmp of moss, see, and ma nest is way on top of a bell twer. So no way could any nrmal brute find it. It was a spook, I reckn.

Me (crafty): No nrmal brute, hem, hem, I see. A spook, hm? Now let me ask Mr. Weasel, did you like yr gld wtch? Also, did you keep it in a silly place like on your frnt doorstp?

Weasel (front toothly): My gld watch was my best thing. It was worth a frtune. I kept it lockd in a chest hid at the btm of a deep dark tunl that I dug for it. No brute knew whr it was, only me. It mst hv been stln by a soopnachrel fors. By the way can you spell s-u-p-e-r-n-a-t-u-r-a-l f-o-r-c-e?

Me (correctingly): Oh, thnks. Now I cn spell it. But what Xactly is a supernatural force, hint, hint?

Weasel: It is 1 of those nsty little green things that I saw come creepn into my bdrm in the drk on the bong of midnit. It was shockn. Would you like a description?

Me: Will I have to take it to the drugstore?

Weasel: I said a DEscription, not a PREscription.

Me: Thank you wunce morely.

Description of "not normal brute,"
"spook," and "nasty thing."

Yours pulltheotheronely,

Little

My mat with all the Supercub pics on it

Dear Mom and Dad,

You say stop doing that silly short writing. You also say my letter made you think of Uncle Bigbad and go all sad and snappish. But listen, why does that supernatural force remind you of Uncle? True, Uncle was a ghost and did glowing in the dark. But he was not 1 bit like the small ratty thing that the weasel saw floating by his nose in the nighttime. Uncle was a great big, tall, horrible ghost when he went haunting. He had a big horrible furry face, plus big horrible red eyes, plus big horrible yellow teeth and streams of dribble dribbling down. Also his eyebrows met in the middle like Dad's, only more caterpillary.

I know Uncle Bigbad got stolen inside his bottle from my house, but serves him right. He should not have eaten so many bakebeans, and then he would not have died of the jumping beanbangs in the first place. And why didn't he stay in the nice grave I dug for him? He would have been safe there. He only moved into that bottle to show off, just because the label had "Powerful Spirit" on it. Then he got corked up and spooknapped by Mister Twister the fox.

So you are 2 crool blaming me for losing him and saying "All Little's fault, he shamed the family name." What about Mister Twister? He is a cunning fox besides being a Wanted Crook. He also is a Master of Dizgizzes (cannot spell it) so he did not leave a trail. And now he has probly buried Uncle miles deep in a faroff land, just for spitefulness. He hates wolves.

Yours suggestingly,

L.B. Wolf (helpful son)

34

Sock drawer

Dear Mom and Dad,

Your Speshal Delivery arrived today, so I got your tape recording of Dad having a go at me. It was very scary, even listening in my sock drawer. I played it 2 times because the 1st time I had socks stuffed 2 far up my ears.

So yes, alright, I am repeating after you, 1) I am a no good detective and not modern enuff.

2) It is a good idea if you want to send Private Investigator Furlock Holmes-Wolf.

3) Yes, I understand. He is going to do some proper investigating and find all the lost small brutes and treasure quick.

4) Also, he will do hi-tech investigating about Uncle Bigbad and bring him back to Frettnin Forest so he can be a proud haunter wunce more and keep up the fierce name of Wolf in Beastshire.

Plus Smells is coming on the train with him and I must be a nice big bro to him and not put him on a leash or in a kennel or anything.

Yours sighingly,

Little

Dear Mom and Dad,

Yesterday I had to go all the way south to Badpenny Junction to meet Furlock Holmes-Wolf and Smells. It was a long trot by myself around Lake Lemming and across Shocking Marshes, so I was a bit late.

Yeller, Stubbs, and Normus are still out looking for missing small brutes. 3 more went missing in the night: 1 otter pup, 1 small squirrel, and 1 earwiggle. Also more brute beasts came in to say they saw the small floaty green glowmouse thing in the night. And when they woke up, their treasure was robbed. But no pawprints or anything.

When I got to the station, I thought, drat, missed them, because the train was going away puffingly in the distance. But no—a big, fat wolf was standing there on the platform. In 1 front paw he was holding a small hard suitcase, and Smell's ted was in the other. What flat feet he's got! Not to mention what a big hat and cape, plus what big glasses! I said, "Hello, you must be Mister Furlock Holmes–Wolf. I am L. Wolf, Esquire, Number 1 cub of Gripper. Also, Co-Cheef Detective of the YFDA."

He said, "Did somebody speak?"

I said, "Yes, me, down here under your big tummy."

He said, "I knew that, actually. Wait there while I work out who you are on my hi-tech laptop machine." Then he opened the suitcase and went *clickerty click, keypad keypad keypad*. Then he said, "Ah, elementary my dear Spotson, you must be Master... er... Knitting Wool."

I said, "No, I am Little Wolf," and he said, "I knew that, actually. The machine is never wrong."

I said, "Excuse me, where is my baby bro and why are you holding his ted's paw?"

He said, "Ted? Don't be ridiculous. Ted is on the luggage rack with my suitcase. See for yourself."

I said, "But Mister Furlock, the train left five minutes ago," and he said, "I just said that, actually!"

Never mind. I xpect Smells will turn up in the Lost and Found office tomorrow.

Yours tuffluckly (only kidding),

Little

Dear Mom and Dad,

Me and Mister Furlock Holmes-Wolf had
to go all the way down to Nasty Bend today
to fetch Smells from the Lost and Found
office there. The guardman made me pay a
big fine for Smells because he did monkey
swings on the emerjuncy string and
pretended to be luggage (plus he ate the
station master's wissul).

Smells was all whiny and
would not walk, so I had
to piggyback him all
the way home with
the hic-wissuls. I also
had to keep picking
up Mister Furlock.
He trips over a lot.
(He is ~~shortsitid~~
~~shirtseated~~ needs
thick glasses.)

40

Yeller, Normus, and Stubbs were waiting for us at the YFDA, but they were all kind of gloomish because of not solving any cases or finding any lost small brutes.

Mister Furlock said, "Aha! That is because of you not being hi-tech. Tomorrow I shall show you sad, small, dim detectives some proper investigating." Then he ate all the supper and got his head stuck in the stewpot.

Your peckish cub,

Little Starver

Dear Mom and Dad,

Mister Holmes-Wolf says we may call him Furlock now, plus he let us have a look at his special investigator power tools.

Here is a pic to show small detectives why using your keen beastly senses is no good:

Technotracker™ – featuring:

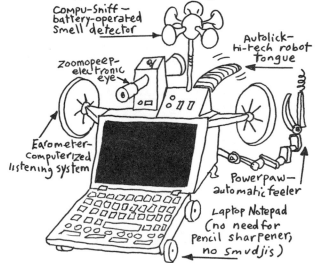

Plus it shows Y using your animal instincts is much 2 old fashy.

Furlock gave us a lesson on how to do automatic sniffing at dinnertime.
He went *clickerty click, keypad keypad keypad.*

Then the machine said (robot voice), "Nasal report! You have a fine cheese on the table. Smellymentary, my dear Watson."

Yeller said, "SORRY TO MENTION IT, BUT MY NOSE REPORTS THERE IS NO CHEESE ON THE TABLE, JUST YOUR FEET, MISTER FURLOCK!"

Furlock said, "I knew that, actually. The keys are a little sticky, that's all."

Furlock says he will do more lessons tomorrow if I pay him 3 gold coins. Handy, because that is just how many Stubbs found in Frettnin Forest the other day. Arrroooo!

Yours Xpectingalottly,

Little

YELLOWEYES FOREST DETECTIVE AGENCY
FRETTNIN FOREST, BEASTSHIRE

Dear Mom and Dad,

    Our lesson today was looking for
Furlock's lost glasses. We spent 3 hours
looking for them with the Technotracker. It
found 1 window, some marbles, 2 jam jars,
and the bathroom mirror. Then Smells went,
har, har, he had them on all the time. He
likes wearing them. He says they make him
feel all funny and giddy.

    Furlock said, "I knew that,
actually. Now I think you
cubs would learn a lot if I told
you how I solved my most
celebrated case, 'The Case of the Slippery
Chicks.' Are you familiar with it?"

    Normus said, "Not really.
You have only told it to
us 15 times."

So Furlock said, "good," and he told us again.

It was wunce upon a cold early springtime. All the wolves up on the hilly end of Lonesome Woods (near your lair) were starving hungry, so they prowled around looking for some tasty snacks to pounce on. Then along came a chicken with 7 chicks. But the wolves could not catch the chicks to eat, because they were much 2 slippery. So they called for Mister Furlock Holmes-Wolf, Investigator, hem, hem. Then off he went crawlingly through the frosty grass, and soonly he came up to a chicken's nest. He pointed his machine at it. And guess what the Technotracker detected? The hen with a butter knife in her beak, spreading margarine on her babies. So he pinched her butter knife. And that was how he became a Faymuss Wolf Hero and Hi-tech Investigator. The end.

Normus did a whisper to me saying, "Hm, I could have spied that hen in just 3 secs, I bet." But Furlock said, "Paws on lips, no talking." Then he told us about some other faymuss cases he solved. "The Case of the Polished Piggies," "The Case of the Hairoiled Hares," "The Case of the Soapy Snakes," "The Case of the Hard-to-Hold Eels," plus "The Case of the Skiddy Sausage Dogs." So boring.

Stubbs said, "Ark! Arkzactly!" meaning aren't these cases arkzactly the same? Yeller said, "YEAH, AREN'T THEY KIND OF. . . IDENTICAL?"

That was when we all got donked on the head with the Technotracker.

Yours bumply,

L. Wolf
P.S. Ouch.

Dear Mom and Dad,

Furlock said I could have a try with the Technotracker if I gave him xtra Moosepops at snack time. He said, "Anyway, you had better test it out in case you damaged it with your heads yesterday."

So I went *clickerty click, keypad keypad keypad,* and the machine said: "Hearing alert! A small mouse just crept in. It chomped up all the Moosepops and removed the cuffs from Investigator Furlock's trousers."

Yeller said, "I THINK THAT MACHINE IS WRONG, BECAUSE THAT MOUSE WAS YOUR BABY BRO."

Normus said, "Hm, try again."

So I went *clickerty click,*
keypad keypad keypad,
and the machine went,
"Nasal alert! The house
is on fire."

Stubbs went, "Ark! Smark!" meaning, Yes,
I smell smark too!

But not really, because guess what? Stubbs
had put furballs in Furlock's pipe, to make a
cozy nest!

Yours coffingly,

L.

P.S. I think the Technotracker is
no good. The YFDA are better clue
hunters (true).

By the big window, staring out (Xcitedly),

Dear Mom and Dad,

Guess what? We had a circus visit from Murkshire today. But then all the animals got kidnapped, so no show, boo, shame. I wanted to see the helifant in case it looks like a helicopter (I like flying).

CIRCUS CANCELED

I am still hopeless at hi-tech work, but here is some GOOD NEWS! You know that small moose that was missing? Stubbs found out he has come back to his herd. Arrroooo! Funny thing is, his antlers have gone all rubbery, so they're not much good for butting with. Ooo-er.

Yours Yzatly?

Little ??????

Dear Mom and Dad,

More good news! All the small lost brutes have been unkidnapped—not just the snacky 1s, but the fierce pouncers too.

They all said the same kind of story, like this: A nice gingery gypsy or minty sweep or knifegrinder came up to them and looked into their eyes saying, softly, softly: "My boys, you must come to my lovely dark den with me." So they went far off from Frettnin Forest.

Then they got put into cages and had to go into a big metal room. Next they had to hold paws and do Ringa Rounda Rosie.

Plus funny sparks started shooting around. Then they all fell down. Then they could not remember. Then they came back to Frettnin Forest to live happy ever after.

Only they are not xactly the same as before. Like the ducklings. If their mom drops a plate and it goes BANG!!, all the ducklings come quacking up quick, saying, "Hello, we like bangs." Also the hedgehogglet has got a zipper under his tummy, so now he can take off his prickles, easy cheesy. All the little rabbits say, "Maa-aa" and won't hide down their holes. Plus they want their mom to knit them white wooly sweaters.

This is funny 2. The lion cub has gone off meat—all he wants are toffee apples.

This looks like a job for THE YFDA! Arrroooo! We are soooooo xcited!

Yours petitly,

Hercule Poireau (french)

P.S. Moi, really.

Dear Mom and Dad,

No, I won't let your darling baby pet go off on his own with any knifegrinder or minty stranger. But tell him not to be such a ~~noosence~~ ~~noosense~~ pain. He keeps switching on the flashlight from our detective kit plus handcuffing the Technotracker.

Yours,

 Senior Boy (hem, hem)

Dear Mom and Dad,

Da-daah! We have a new case!

A hermit came knocking at our door today saying, "Good day, I would like to speak to a detective."

I was just going to say, "Hello, I am Little Wolf, Co-Cheef Detective," but Furlock said buttinnly, "You are fortunate. Please enter. Allow me to introduce myself. Furlock Holmes-Wolf, celebrated Hi-Tech Investigator at your service."

The hermit came in with a cloak on. He had sharp eyes, big boots, plus rubber gloves. Also he smelled of catnip and his trousers were all bunchy at the back. He said (hermitly), "Good morrow. I am a just a poor old hermit. I live in a woodcutter's cottage by myself and last night I was visited by a horrid green spookly thing. I have nothing to rob, but I fear I shall be kidnapped. I need protecting. Is that part of your YFDA service?"

Furlock said, "Fear no more, old hermit. 3 of my young helpers— Yeller, Normus, and Smellybreff—will protect you. I personally shall bring my faithful Technotracker to investigate the green intruder."

Yeller said, "GOOD. I LIKE PROTECTIN'."

Normus said, "Yes, and I like bashing intruders."

I said, "Hey, do not forget me and Stubbs."

So Furlock said, "Little Wolf and Stubby Crow will remain here in case of emerjuncies."

Then Smells started whining, saying he was not going, he hated woodcutters' huts. But then the hermit's sharp eyes went wide and he said softly, "My boy, something tells me that you are a keen young laddie who is eager to assist an old hermit in his difficulties." Smells did not know how to say no to him. So off they all went in a small pack.

Oh boo. I hate staying at home. Not fair.

Yours fedduply,

Littly

Dear Mom and Dad,

Stubbs and me waited and waited all night, but no emerjuncies for us—boo, shame.

At sunjump we wanted to be busy, so we ran rushingly on the trail with our magnifying glasses. We followed the boot and pawprints for many a minute and many an hour, because it went all zigzaggy. But that did not put us off. After long searching in the deep dark forest, we found the wood-cutter's hut in a clearing. It was just on the north edge of Frettnin Forest (you could see Windy Ridge behind). In we went boldly, but—oh no! It was all empty. We looked around sadly, then out came my detective kit notebook and sharp pencil. I stuck on my Clues sticker and wrote this:

CLUES

- 🐾 1 big room, few books, big fireplace, not much ~~fernichure funnychir~~ chairs etc.
- 🐾 lots of rope (very sticky)
- 🐾 1 Technotracker — bashed to bits on floor
- 🐾 1 smushed-up piece of paper (nothing on it)
- 🐾 large rubber gloves
- 🐾 bunches of dandylion stalks with seeds blown off
- 🐾 1 of these

Then we went hurryingly outside again to look for a new trail. Stubbs did Air Searching, but we could only find the trail we came by, not 1 other whiff or print! Where has everybody gone?

Yours scratchheadly,
  Little ????

Dear Mom and Dad,

Now the Technotracker is dead, me and Stubbs must do our detecting the good old fashy way (lots of brute instinct, plus use keen beastly senses, etc., remember?).

So Stubbs unsmushed the paper. He made it nice and flat and laid it on the floor, but no writing on it.

Next he started poking his clever beak into the books while I had a good sniff and lick around the room, thinking, Hmmm, all that funny rope. Y is it so thick and sticky? What is that metal thing called a HE? Y are there no fingerprints of the hermit, because I can see loads of pawprints of Furlock, Yeller, Normus, and Smells?

Also, I could smell all the different smells of them, plus a strong scent of catnip. I said outloudly, "Hmm, catnip, let me see . . ." and all of a suddenly, Stubbs said, "Ark!" meaning look what I have found in the enzarkclopedia!

He showed me how somebody had turned down the corner of 1 page, at letter C for **catnip**. Quick as a chick, I read the words on the page:

Catnip: **A fine smelly plant loved by cats and other cunning pouncers. The smell is strong enough to cover up all kinds of other strong scents, including parsley, mint, rosemary, thyme, and**

And guess what? On the word *pepper* there was a pawprint. "That is a foxprint!" I xclaimed. Stubbs went, "Ark!" meaning arkstraordinary detecting work.

And which fox would go, "Pepper! Yessss!" and poke the word with his paw? Stubbs went, "Ark," meaning it is arksactly the same fox who would dress up as a gypsy, knife-grinder, or hermit.

Answer: **Mister Twister!**

Smellymintery, my dear parentals!

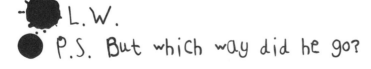

L.W.

P.S. But which way did he go?

Dear Mom and Dad,

2 branes are better than 1, that is Y Stubbs and me are good workouters.

Stubbs went to have a good look up the chimney, so I had a close look at the funny metal thing with HE on it. It had a little tap, so I gave it a turn and it went FSSSSSSHH!

So scary!

So in my notebook I wrote . . .

SOLVED MYSTERIES

Who was that hermit?

Answer: Mister Twister, cunning fox and master of Dizgizzes (cannot spell it) ✓

Y did he have bunchy trousers at the back?

Answer: to hide his bushy red tail ✓

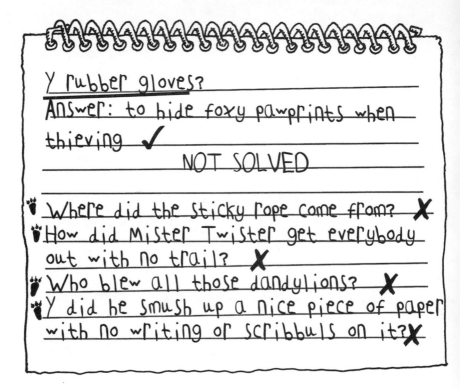

Y rubber gloves?
Answer: to hide foxy pawprints when thieving ✓

NOT SOLVED

🐾 Where did the sticky rope come from? ✗
🐾 How did Mister Twister get everybody out with no trail? ✗
🐾 Who blew all those dandylions? ✗
🐾 Y did he smush up a nice piece of paper with no writing or scribbuls on it? ✗

Wait—Stubbs has come back down the chimney saying, "Ark!" meaning he is all arkscited. Must find out Y. Will write again soonly.

Yours investigately,

Little

P.S. Do you know an investigator is an alligator in a vest (not really—joke to stop you going sob, where is our baby?)

Dear Mom and Dad,

Good thing Stubbs
got nice and sooty,
because he landed
on that unsmushed
piece of paper and
had a good shake.
It was like a
magic thing,
because letters
came up on the
paper! I will tell
you Y. Because of
someone (Mister
Twister) using it to
lean on when he was
doing heavy writing on
another piece of paper on top.
Get it? He made all dents and lines, and
when they got sooty they looked like this:

The Hermitage, Woodcutter's Cottage, The Clearing, Frettnin Forest, Beastshire

My Dear Bookseller,

I like reading a great deal. Rush me the following books that interest me strangely.

**EXPERIMENTING WITH ANIMALS
by Ken U. Alterum
MUCKING AROUND WITH GENES
by I. M. Rich
HOW TO BUILD YOUR OWN GENETIC
MODIFICATION CHAMBER
by Ivor Startupp-Kitt**

Yours urgently,

A. Hermit

Stubbs went, "Arks," meaning arkstraordinary, is that how you spell "jeans"? But we found Genetic Modification in the enzarklopedia. It said it means changing things by messing with their insides. That is a bit 2 hard for us, because we are only small. So what is that cunning fox up to?

But now clever Stubbs has detected how Mister Twister got away. I will tell you later, but Stubbs is saying "Ark!" meaning arkscuse him. He wants me to help him quick. He is making something with his clever beak. It is good.

Yours bizzybeely,

Buzzy

Dear Mom and Dad,

What do you think? I am sending you this nice pic of our airship we made in the nighttime. We made it out of the sticky rope, the wastepaper basket, and a rubber glove blown up with FSSSSSSSH out of the metal thing with HE on it. (If you turn it around it says LIUM on its back. HE + LIUM = gas for blowing up balloons and airships! We looked that up in the enzarklopedia too!) Arrroooo!

Now I s'pect you will say, Little Wolf, what are you up 2 now? Answer: flying north-north-eastly on the trail of Mister Twister. But you will say, Little, do not be such a guesser. How can you tell Mister Twister went away airly? Also, how can you tell which way he went?

Answer, *helium-entary,* my dear Mom and Dad! Because:

1) Stubbs has done big Air Searches lately, meaning he knows the wind here is a north-north-east 1.

2) He found lots of pawprints going just 1 way.

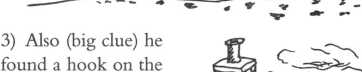

3) Also (big clue) he found a hook on the chimney saying "Airship Hook" on it.

4) He found lots more dandylions with the seeds blown off. That was a hard puzzle, but we did a shut-your-eyes-and-think-squeezingly. All of a suddenly, Stubbs said, "Ark!" meaning eurarka, I have found out something!

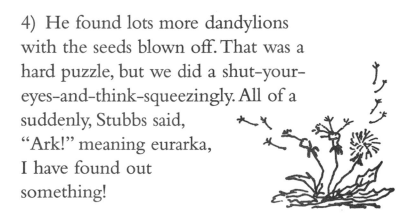

I said, "What?" Answer: Mister Twister was holding up dandylions to find out *how* strong the wind was blowing and *which way!* So, well done, our Flying Squad!

Your breezy boy,

L.W.

P.S. Hmm, flying. Nice.

On some rocky ground, Dark Hills

Dear Mom and Dad,

We have landed bonkingly near Broken Tooth Caves. Stubbs wanted to let all the FSSSSSH out with a sharp peck. But I said no, save it for later. So we hid the airship behind a big rock. Now it is very dark, but Stubbs is holding the flashlight in his clever beak so I can do my writing. Good we had our detective kit with us.

The paths around here are rocky, so no pawprints. But we found 1 good clue:

This is a button from Smells's sailor suit, so he is probably kidnapped and in a cave. With the others, I bet. BUT (big but) which cave? There are so many!

It is creepy here. My beastly instinct has gone all tickly, like when I see a big hairy spider. There must be lots of spiders very close by.

OOOOOOOOoooooOOOOOOoooo !

What was that? A loud trumpet noise!
Sorry about the smudjis. All's quiet now. We are starving. Wish I had 1 of Mom's rabbit rolls or a tasty mice pie, yum, yum! I will have to look for emerjuncy rations instead.

Yours rummagingly,

Littly

Behind a big rock, by Broken Tooth Caves,
Dark Hills

Dear Mom and Dad,

Did I say we were both starving hungry and wishing for Mom's rabbit rolls, yum, yum? Well, I got out my emerjuncy matchbox to see if I had any tasty crawlers in it for crunchy snacks. It was empty, boo, shame. So we took out our magnifying glasses, and off we went searchingly in the crooks and nannies. (Other way around, sorry.)

We searched and searched. My yellow eyes made friends with the dark, but then

HELP!
TYRANOSAURUS
REX!

Yours panickly,

The Wizzer

Dear Mom and Dad,

You want to be careful with magnifying glasses. Sometimes they do tricks to trick you, because you know that T-rex? It was a stick insect really. The magnifying glass was just pretending.

Never mind, because guess what? The stick insect jumped in my matchbox. So handy! I was just going to give it a nibble, but Stubbs said, "Ark," meaning that is arkstraordinary! Y did the stick insect just hop in your matchbarks like that?

So I said, "Tell me, Mister Crunchy Snack, how did you learn to do hopping so high?" And the insect said (stickly), "I learned it from a cricket. I had to hold hands with him and do a Ringa Rounda Rosie in the metal room that went all sparky."

I said, "Ooo-er. I have heard that Ringa
Rounda Rosie story before. Were you by any
chance captured by a foxy hermit? Or a
minty knifegrinder? Or a gingery gypsy?"

The sticky said back, "Yes, I was! But
I . . ." Stubbs said, "Ark!" meaning, you
arkscaped.

The sticky said, "My, what a clever cub and
crowchick you are. You should be detectives."

I said a proud aha. "Aha! We *are*
detectives. We are from the YFDA. And that
foxy kidnapper was none other than Mister
Twister, Master of Dizzgizzes (cannot spell it)
and most-wanted crook of Frettnin Forest.
Now tell us what happened, because I am
always ready, and my pencil is a sharp 1."

Yours notingly,

L.

Huge big dark place, Broken Tooth Caves,
Dark Hills

Dear Mom and Dad,

We have made friends with Sticky. He is
nice and a good watcher, so no eating him.
(Lucky Stubbs shared his wiggly grubs with
me, so my tummy is not 2 rumbly now.)
Sticky says he has seen lots of cages here.
They are full of captured brute beasts, some
big, some small. All sorts. The biggest 1 is
gray, like a big wrinkly house with 4 legs. It
has ears like car doors, plus a hosepipe in the
front for tunes and for suctioning you up.
Maybe that is the helifant that got kidnapped
from the circus. Maybe it was him who made
us jump with his loud trumpet.

Also, Sticky say that sometimes Mister Twister carries a bottle. He holds it up like a lantern when he goes walking in the dark tunnels and looking in the cages. He says it shines with a green glow. Oh no! I think that green glowness is the ghost of Uncle Bigbad! So shaming to end up as a lamp for a fox!

1 other bad thing is that Mister Twister has got 2 terrible creatures to guard the cages all the time. They are as big as cats and fierce, with 8 furry legs like spiders! They made all that sticky rope, I bet! No wonder my fur feels tickly all the time. Spiders are my worst thing (xcept for loud bangs).

Sticky told us that the last things Mister Twister captured were 4 cocoons, like silkworms. 1 was a big, fat cocoon. Another was big and furry. 1 was small and loud. Then there was a small 1 with a sailor hat on. That is Furlock, Normus, Yeller, and Smells, I bet—captured by the hermit. Sticky says they are locked up in the Hall of Cages, near the metal room that goes sparky, and guarded by spidercat guards.

Sticky wants to come rescuing with us. He wants to save his chum the cricket, because he cannot jump away himself. Good, huh?

Stubbs said, "Ark!" meaning do not worry, we will help the crarket to arkscape!

Pawscrossedly for luck,

Little cheef

Dear Mom and Dad,

We are in Broken Tooth Caves. It is drippy and ploppy and has so many tunnels. But Sticky has good feelers for finding the way in the darkness. We must not use Stubby's flashlight (2 giveaway), so I am writing this in glowworm juice. Hope U can read it.

Wait—we have found the Hall of Cages. It is quiet. We can hear small snores. That is a mouse snore. That is a badger, and a ferret, and a squirrel! Tippy on the toes. Wait—my nose is telling me. Yes! I smell a baby bro. He is near. I must use my keenly senses. Wish my yellow eyes were *more* keen.

Ooo-er! There is Smells in his little cocoon—very still, no wiggling! Also Yeller, Normus, and Furlock all tied up tight. And such a big lock on the cage door.

Oh no, help! Stubbs has been pounced on!

Yours panickly,

By a plughole

Dear Mom and Dad,

It was Mister Twister's Spidercat
Guards! Huge meowing spiders—help! They
came swinging from the roof on their sticky
ropes. Stubbs gave 1 a hard peck, but they
were 2 strong and tied him up spinningly.

Up went my fur, all tickly on my back. That
was my beastly instinct saying 2 me, *Look out
behind you, Little!* I went flat, but then Stubbs
called, "Ark!" meaning fire arkstinguisher! It
was by me on the wall.

Bang I went on the button, and out came
the water with a SHUSHHHHH! Har, har,
that was a good skwirter. I shouted, "Put

your legs up, you Spidercats! I
am a proud detective
wolf, so you are under
arrest. Give me the
keys to the cages."
They tried to pounce
on me swiftly. So I
skwirted and skwirted
them right in the nasty
eyes and right in the nasty
teeth. I chased them along the Hall of Cages
till they came to a big drainhole, and
DOWN they went
wooshingly. And
guess what?
The keys
dropped out
of their
horrible mouths!

Yours servumrightly,

  Sir Skwirtalot Wolf

Hall of Cages, Broken Tooth Caves

Dear Mom and Dad,

I got the penknife out of my Detective Kit and cut Stubbs free. Then we unlocked the cage and Stubbs got busy with his clever beak. All the sticky rope was in heaps on the floor before you could say a kwick thing like, "Hello everybody, we have come to save you."

Yeller said, "WELL DONE, LITTLE AND STUBBS." But Smells gave me a sharp nip, and Furlock said, "I knew you would come, actually. Did you find us by my Technotracker?"

I said, "No we found you by our eyes, noses, and other beastly senses, because we are the YFDA. And the Technotracker is defnly a TechNOtracker now. It was Mister Twister who did the smashing up."

He said, "What? Did you say smashing up? TSO! TSO! Quick!"

Normus said, "What is TSO—is it bashing?"

Furlock said, "TSO is Trot Swiftly Off! NOW!"

I said, "But we have nearly found out WHODUNNIT and WHATFOR. And we have to rescue Uncle Bigbad's ghost. And what about freeing the other brute beasts and arresting Mister Twister?"

Furlock said, "Frankly, I do not care a flea WHODUNNIT or WHATFOR, or for Bigbad Wolf either. He is far too wild for my liking. I intend to TSO before anyone thinks of smashing *me* up. If you have any sense, you will join me while you still can. Good-bye. Whoops." And off he rushed, trippingly. He was only wurrid about saving himself.

Yours leftinthelurchly,

THE YFDA

Dear Mom and Dad,

Pity about Furlock, huh? Ask Dad to give him a good nip the next time he sees him. Yeller said, "GOOD RIDDANCE TO HIM! AND WELL DONE, CHUMS! YOU SAVED US. THAT CRAFTY FOX WAS GOIN' TO EXPERIMENT ON US TODAY. HE WAS GOIN' TO PUT US IN HIS METAL ROOM. HE SAID WE ARE THE LAST PART OF HIS CUNNIN' PLAN."

GRRR

Normus said, "Yes, well done, fellers! Now we can do some bashing at last!"

I said, "No bashing yet, Normus. 1st we must find out Mister Twister's cunning plan. Where is he?"

Yeller said, "HE IS IN A LOCKED ROOM TALKIN' INTO HIS TAPE RECORDER."

I said, "Then we must use our keenly senses to find out what he is saying."

Normus said, "Shame we don't have an electronic listening device like Furlock had. We could bug the room with that."

That made Yeller have 1 of his Big Ideers. He said, "BUG-AMENTARY, MY DEAR NORMUS! WE WILL PUT A BUG IN TO LISTEN. BUT NO NEED FOR ELECTRIC!"

Sticky said bravely, "I'm a bug. Will I do?" But Stubbs said, "Ark!" meaning what about your friend the craket? He would be even better.

Time for Hunt the Cricket. Arrroooo!

Yours eagerly,

The YFDA

Dim Tunnel, Broken Tooth Caves

Dear Mom and Dad,

It did not take long finding the cricket.
He was in a jam jar close by. He was a bit
wurrid about getting chomped, but then he
was happy to be a detective bug for us.

We went shushly along the dark Hall of
Cages. Soonly we found a big strong door
saying TOP SECRET—CRAFTY
FOXES ONLY! Quick as a chick, we
popped the cricket in the keyhole so
he could see and hear that cunning
crook and kidnapper Mister Twister.
Plus he could talk to us, by rubbing his
legs together chirpingly. Good, huh?

Yours spyly,

 Little Eye

By the keyhole of the Secret Room,
Broken Tooth Caves

Dear Mom and Dad,

Here is the cricket news (translated by
Sticky—he speaks cricket best). This was
spoken softly into a tape recorder by Mister
Twister about his secret Xperiments!

**"Crafty Plan, Code Name PYOF.
Listening Diary of My Crafty Self, Day
43.** Testing, testing. Hello, dear boy. As I speak
today, my Master Plan is almost complete, so I
shall give myself the pleasure of
summing up my remarkable
achievement. My first
brilliant stroke was to
kidnap my rival in crime,
the once great and terrible
Bigbad Wolf. The label on
the bottle where he resides reads
"Powerful Spirit." What nonsense that seems
now—ha ha—he is my pet, my slave. And

88

why must he do all that I command? Simple! "The answer is pinned to my chest. It is a well known fact that he who dares to snatch a single hair from the tail of a wolf shall master him forever—and I have his entire tail! How? By craft and cunning, for I knew that the wretch had blown himself to pieces as a result of eating bakebeans too fast. I also discovered that the only part of him that his pesky nephew, Little Wolf, could find to bury was his whiskers. So patiently I searched and snuffed, never giving up until I had tracked down the tail that has made my fortune!

"Knowing that ghosts can always find hidden stores of gold and jewels, my first command to him was to keep his miniature shape and size, and to do all my treasure seeking. That allowed me time to kidnap at least 1 small brute of every species in Frettnin Forest. And to study.

"Very soon I taught my sharp self the science of genetic modification, for I wished to change the kidnapped creatures for the better. Better for me, that is! My aim was to turn them into convenience food! Once Bigbad had stolen enough treasure to allow me to do so, I purchased a beautiful machine —my metal box—my Genetic Modification Chamber! After that, I began my Great Plan, Code Name PYOF! It has been a huge success and is almost complete. I am switching off now in order to carry out my final Master Stroke!"

Oh no! He is coming out. . . .

Yours hidingly,

L.

Dear Mom and Dad,

We all went back gaspingly to the Hall of Cages. Cricket's legs were stiff from so much chirping, but we all had to use our keen beastly senses quick! This is our plan:

1) Sticky and Cricket—take keys and open up all the cages

2) Me and Stubbs—hide high up in the shadows

3) Normus, Yeller, and Smells— pretend to be tied up again in their cage

4) Get a big, fat sack so it looks like Furlock is in the cage 2.

I will tell you the rest if it works.

Yours riskingly,

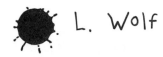 L. Wolf

P.S. If not, good-bye forever, Mom and Dad. We tried our best. Call the Murkshire Wolf Pack and get ready to fight against Mister Twister before he gets you 2.

Dear M and D,

Not dead, but nearly—phew! I will tell
you what happened:

Up lit the hall with the green glow of
Uncle Bigbad. Mister Twister was holding
Uncle up by his bottle to light the way. He
was speaking into his tape recorder again,
saying softly:

"Listening Diary, Day 43, continued.
As I was saying, my Master Plan is
to turn Frettnin Forest into a
PYOF, or Pounce on Your
Own Forest! I shall soon be
able to feast on all my favorite
creatures with no danger to
myself whatsoever! My prey will be
easy, and my enemies will be feeble and
powerless against me! I shall grow gorgeously
fat and sleek and never have a single worry.

"Using my GM chamber, I have mixed up the shapes and habits of my kidnap victims, large and small. Already I have created a vegetarian lion by crossing him with a lamb. I  have crossed a pheasant with a bird dog, so that it runs toward hunters. I have crossed a hedgehog with a knapsack  so that I can unzip his prickles and have a deliciously instant snack.

"A piggy has been crossed with a rabbit so that he  will pop straight into the cooking pot, crying 'Lucky me, I have found my burrow!' A shy little mouse has been crossed with a hyena, so now I can hear him laughing,  no matter how tall the grass is where he hides.

"One by one I am returning these changed creatures to their homes. Only yesterday I sent back a young squirrel. His mother is wondering why he is terrified of heights and will not climb up to his nest. She has no idea that I have crossed him with a mole!

"Now, as a special treat for myself, I have saved the best experiment till last. I intend to cross some meddling wolves and an interfering young bear with a litter of poodle pups. After just 30 seconds playing Ringa Rounda Rosie in my GM Chamber, they will all be tamed. They will roll over on their backs and let me tickle their tummies! Spidercat guards, bring out the prisoners!"

Help!
Yours tobecontinuedly,

The proud cubs
of Frettnin Forest

Dear M and D,

Har har, hee hee, I love having my tummy tickled by a crafty fox (not really, only kidding).

We had a nice BIG shock for Mister Twister. Me and Stubbs were The Flying Squad. We came dropping quick out of the roof shadows. Down we whooshed swingingly on a sticky rope. I put out my paws like an X and Stubbs sat on my head and made an X with his legs and wings. So when Mister Twister saw our shadow coming, he thought we were a Spidercat guard!

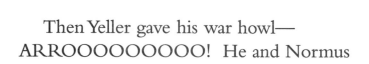

Then Yeller gave his war howl— ARROOOOOOOOOO! He and Normus

and Smells threw their ropes off, opened their cage, and charged snappingly at the vain and peppery plotter. Mister Twister tried to bash them with his tape recorder, but I kept swinging and knocked him over with a flying kick. That was when Stubbs grabbed Uncle Bigbad's bottle in his clever beak and flew away with it.

And guess what I got with my clever paw? Uncle's tail!

Sticky and Cricket were good unlockers. Out came all the kidnapped creatures chargingly. They butted and pecked and bashed and bit and gave that fox a good noisy fight. The helifant made his scariest trumpet noise and did a lot of nice squashing and squishing and swishing with his hosepipe. He was sooooo Xcited to be out of his cage!

But he lost his way in the darkness and got himself stuck in the GM Chamber, boo, shame.

That made Mister Twister get his cunningness up again. He turned his foxy eyes on us saying, "Now my boys, stop all this roughness. Just look deep deeeep into my eyes and do what I command." Good thing my brute instinct called out to Stubbs, "Quick! Throw the bottle to the helifant." So he did a swift loop the loop. Then the helifant's hosepipe reached up and sucked the bottle out of his beak. I banged the door shut and switched the switch, *click.*

The chamber started to shake and spark and rock as the helifant did Ringa Rounda Rosie with the ghost of Uncle Bigbad. Then

The chamber door flew off and

CRACKLE FLASH FUME

Out came flying the faymuss Terror of
Haunted Hall. It was the good old
ghost of Uncle Bigbad, back to his
normal monster size! He had his
great big, horrible red eyes and
his great big, horrible yellow
teeth, and all his horrible dribble
dribbling down. Arrrooooo!

Yours victori–ussly,

The YFDA

P.S. I have done a nice pic
of Mister Twister with a
bashed up tail and lots
of lumps running
away limply.

Safely home again

Dear Mother and Father of mine,

I ~~reseaved~~ ~~receeved~~ ~~received~~ got your letter saying Furlock came around to the Lair going moan groan, no more hi-tech investigating for him. He is opening a fix-it-up shop for sad wolves that keep tripping up and bumping their knees. And it is all my fault.

You say I am a bad boy because I did not let Smells do handcuffing on Mister Twister, he wanted to do that spesh. So now he is all upset. Also you say I must spoil your darling baby ~~pest~~ pet more, like letting him get cubnapped and tied up more often because those are his favorites. You say let him have more ruff fun and give in to him all the time, it is the only way.

100

Har har, I know that is just your wolfly way to say well done, and pat pat for cunningness.

Also you mean to say congrat-arroooshuns for solving lots of tricky cases all at wunce by trying hard, plus normal wolfly sense and brute instinct. Plus doing all that rescuing and saving Frettnin Forest from being a Pounce on Your Own Forest for one fat fox.

You are sooo nice, hem, hem, joke.

Yours proud and Co-Cheefly,

Moi (French)

YELLOWEYES FOREST DETECTIVE AGENCY
FRETTNIN FOREST, BEASTSHIRE

My office, a long time later

Dear Mom and Dad,

Since my last letter, The YFDA has done a lot of genetic unmodification on the kidnapped brute beasts that got put in the chamber. Because we want Frettnin Forest back to its normal wild self. Also we wanted Uncle to go back to his proper happy haunting ground and keep up the terrible name of Wolf. Arrroooo! (I have given him back his tail but, guess what? Ssshhh, I kept 1 small hair, just in case I need to boss him around. Because then if Yeller and Normus and me want to be pirates or spacecubs, he might come in handy, yesss?)

Your busy boy,

L. Wolf
Co-Cheef Detective YFDA

No, Mom and Dad, I do not mean be like peabugs. This is your in vitayshun to come and see our mini circus. It is a BIG THRILL!

I have made you a pic of SMELLYBREFF THE CLOWN doing a skwirt with his HELIFANTEDDY. He made the helifant do Ringa Rounda Rosie with his ted, before we put wheels on the GM Chamber and turned it into a nice caravan. Cozy, hmmmm. . . .

Sticky and Cricket wanted to stay being modified, so now they can be THE AMAZING JUMPING TINY T-REX AND HIS FRIEND THE CRICKET ON STILTS.

The helifant likes being shrunk best 2. It is good because he is a nice attraction. He can play his trumpet and also be THE WORLD'S ONLY HELIFANT IN A BOTTLE.

Also we have THE WORLD'S LOUDEST RINGMASTER, YELLER WOLF! And Normus is our STRONGEST BEAR CUB EVER!

Stubbs and me are trapezers called THE FLYING SPIDERCATS.

You'll have a ball, come one and come all.

Yours swingingly,

Little Bigtop

ARROOOOOOOOOO!!!